For my dad
- Mr. Jay

New Paige Press, LLC
NewPaigePress.com

Copyedited by Amanda Brodkin

ISBN 978-0-692-15613-1

Printed and bound in China

New Paige Press provides special discounts when purchased in larger volumes for premiums and promotional purposes, as well as for fundraising and educational use. Custom editions can also be created for special purposes. In addition, supplemental teaching material can be provided upon request. For more information, please contact sales@newpaigepress.com.

The Bear and the Fern

Written by Mr. Jay • Illustrated by Mary Manning

It started one day, when a man and his wife,
moved into a house to begin their new life.
They laid down the carpets, and painted one wall.
They hung up some pictures in the front entry hall.

Their family came over,
bringing gifts for their home —
three blenders, two toasters
and a used garden gnome.

And one, final gift
that they liked quite a lot —
a smallish green plant
in a reddish clay pot.

The plant was placed down, near a window with care,
in a room with a crib, and a brand new stuffed bear
with brilliant white fur, and a wide, happy grin,
like he just couldn't wait for the fun to begin.

The bear woke each night and snuck out the door,
anxious to run 'round the house and explore.

He'd ask the plant nicely, each night 'fore he went,
"Care to go for a walk?" but she'd never consent.
"I can't go, don't bother," said the plant, sounding stern,
"I'm not able to move, I'm only a fern."
        "But won't you just try?" Bear sounded confused.
        But Fern shook her leaves as she firmly refused.

So Bear, with a sigh, would explore on his own,
while Fern watched the yard, through the glass, all alone.

Weeks rolled on by, and Fern wouldn't relent,
secure in her place, unmoved and content,
while Bear ran off playing with new friends he had made —
a vacuum, some books, and a pale pink lampshade.

He'd ask every night,
before roaming about,
"Could we go for a walk?
It's so nice to go out!"
There's a garden out back,
and it all smells so sweet,
with some funny old roses
that I'd like you to meet."

And each time he'd ask, Fern would soundly reject,
"I'm a potted houseplant, what *do* you expect?
Plants sit and we grow, and we take in the sun.
We don't walk, we don't spin, we don't have that much fun."

"But how do you know? Try it once!" he'd implore.
But Fern wouldn't budge from her place on the floor.

Months passed them by, and the days became colder,
Bear's fur had faded, and Fern had grown older.
Each night, Bear'd go out, whether snow, cold, or rain,
while Fern watched him play, from behind her glass pane.
And night after night, he'd ask Fern to go,
but each time he'd ask, she'd just shake her leaves, "No."

Seasons flew by, and years faded away,
with Fern in her spot, and Bear out to play.
His one ear was chewed, and his fur matted down.
Her leaves had grown bigger, and some edges were brown.

But still Bear kept trying, "You don't need to be prone,"
and Fern would snap back, "Just leave me alone."

Decades would pass
in much the same way,
and then, as it happened,
on one fateful day,
a strange man appeared
and came through the door,
and dropped a big box
in the room, on the floor.

He packed up the box with all that could fit,
some toys, a few games and a used catcher's mitt.
He moved out the bed, the dresser and chair,
then on top of the box, he placed the old bear.
"I've no room for this plant," the man said with a bark,
and he left Fern behind, on her spot, in the dark.

Fern sat real still in the silence of night,
reflecting upon her unfortunate plight.
The only light came from a bit of moonglow,
and she anxiously looked through the frosty window.

But no one was playing, in the cold, wintry air,
and she wept as she realized that bear wasn't there.

Then, all alone, her leaves withered and dry,
Fern sadly wondered, "Well, what if I try?"
She rocked to her left, then swayed to the right,
pushing herself with all of her might.
It took all of her strength, and the last of her will...
but she took a small hop away from the sill.

She couldn't believe it, and started to cry.
"I knew you could do it, if only you'd try."
It was Bear! He'd come back, and he stood at the door,
more faded, more brilliant, than ever before.

"I'm sorry," said Fern, as she finished a spin,
"I'm sorry I waited so long to begin."

Bear hobbled over to Fern's brand new spot,
and put his arm gently around the clay pot.
"Come, Fern," Bear whispered, too choked up to talk,
"Come, take my hand, and let's go for a walk."

ABOUT THE AUTHOR
JAY MILETSKY

Father, author, and business owner, Jay is excited to begin a new career
bringing positive, happy, and sometimes heartwarming stories to children
and their families. He graduated from Brandeis University and currently
lives in New Jersey, where his daughter, Bria Paige, is the inspiration for
all of his creative writing endeavors.

To book Jay for a speaking engagement and to see his upcoming book
titles, please visit jaymiletsky.com